COUNT ON CULEBRA

Go from 1 to 10 in Spanish

by

ANN WHITFORD PAUL

illustrated by

ETHAN LONG

Holiday House / New York

To my favorite doctors,
Henya and Ron
A. W. P.

For Mark and Amy Hinson
E. L.

Text copyright © 2008 by Ann Whitford Paul
Illustrations copyright © 2008 by Ethan Long
All Rights Reserved
Printed and Bound in China
The text typeface is Barcelona Book.
The illustrations were done in gouache
and colored pencil.
www.holidayhouse.com
First Edition
1 3 5 7 9 10 8 6 4 2

Library of Congress Cataloging-in-Publication Data
Paul, Ann Whitford.
Count on Culebra : go from 1 to 10 in Spanish /
by Ann Whitford Paul ;
illustrated by Ethan Long. — 1st ed.
p. cm.
Summary: When Iguana stubs her toe and
cannot make her popular candies known as
cactus butter dulces, Culebra the rattlesnake
finds a cure that introduces the Spanish words
for the numbers from one to ten.
ISBN-13: 978-0-8234-2124-4 (hardcover)
[1. Iguanas—Fiction. 2. Rattlesnakes—Fiction.
3. Snakes—Fiction. 4. Desert animals—Fiction.
5. Counting. 6. Spanish language—Fiction.]
I. Long, Ethan, ill. II. Title.
III. Title: Go from one to ten in Spanish.
PZ7.P278338Co 2008
[E]—dc22
2007017303

Iguana stumbled on a stone.

"OWWWWWWWW!" she cried.

Tortuga poked out of his shell. "What's wrong?"

"I stubbed my toe. It hurts to stand."

Iguana flopped down on her boulder.

"Now I can't make my *dulces*."

"Your yummy cactus butter candies!" Tortuga said.
"That's terrible. Let me rub your toe."
"Stop," moaned Iguana. "You're making it worse."
Conejo hopped over. "I can help."
He wrapped a cloth around Iguana's toe.
"Now you can make cactus butter *dulces*."
"My toe still hurts," Iguana said.
"I'll have to make my *dulces* another day."

"ANOTHER DAY!" Culebra squirmed close.
"This calls for Doctor Culebra."
"When did you go to medical school?"
asked Tortuga.
Conejo snickered.
"You're no doctor."

"You'll see."
Culebra shook
his rattle.
"I know the perfect
cure for Iguana's toe.
First I need a rope."

"A rope?"
asked Tortuga.
"Some doctor!"
But he fetched
Culebra a long one.

"Tie the rope
   onto Iguana's tail,"
   said Culebra.
"My tail doesn't hurt!"
   cried Iguana.
"My toe does!"
"Do what I say,"
   said Culebra.
"I told you he
   wasn't a doctor,"
   said Conejo.

Culebra shook his rattle louder.
"And you," he said to Conejo, "tie *un* rolling pin and *dos* kettles onto the rope."

Conejo tied the rolling pin and kettles onto the rope. "Now we need *tres* skillets," said Culebra.

Tortuga tied them onto the rope. "What kind of doctor would use *tres* skillets?"

"Do you want Iguana's cactus butter *dulces*?" asked Culebra. Everyone nodded.

"Then bring *cuatro* pots.
  Cinco pans will help too."
"No more," said Iguana.
"Yes, more!" Culebra hissed.
"Doctor's orders."

Conejo tied *cuatro* pots and *cinco* pans to the rope.
"*Uno, dos, tres, cuatro, cinco,*" Iguana counted.
"*Cinco* is enough."

"*Cinco* is not nearly enough," he said.
"*Seis* pie tins AND *siete* cups are necessary."
"Necessary for what?" asked Tortuga.
Culebra raised himself high.
"Necessary for *dulces*."

Tortuga hurried to tie
on *seis* pie tins and
siete cups.
"Next, *ocho* knives,
please."

"This is crazy," cried Iguana
as Conejo tied on
ocho knives.

"We're almost done,"
said Culebra,
squirming closer.
"Tie on *nueve* forks,
Tortuga, and
diez spoons."

Tortuga fastened them onto the rope.
Then they all counted,
*"Uno, dos, tres, cuatro, cinco, seis, siete,
ocho, nueve, diez."*
"That should be plenty," said Culebra.
"Some cure," said Iguana. "My toe doesn't
feel one bit better."
"Ahhhhh, but we're not done," said Culebra.
"Now you must walk."
"With this heavy rope?"
"Doctor Culebra's orders," he said.

Iguana took a step.

CLINK, CLANK, CLANG thumped the rolling pin and kettles.

KLATTER, KLITTER, KLING bumped the skillets, pots, and pans.
"I feel foolish," said Iguana.

PLINK, PLANK, PLANG rapped
the pie tins and the cups.
BLATTER, BLITTER, BLING
tapped the knives and forks and spoons.
"Too much noise!"
complained Iguana.
"Keep walking," said Culebra.

CLINK, CLANK, CLANG,
KLATTER, KLITTER, KLING,
PLINK, PLANK, PLANG,
BLATTER, BLITTER, BLING

"Walk faster," ordered
Culebra. "Much faster."

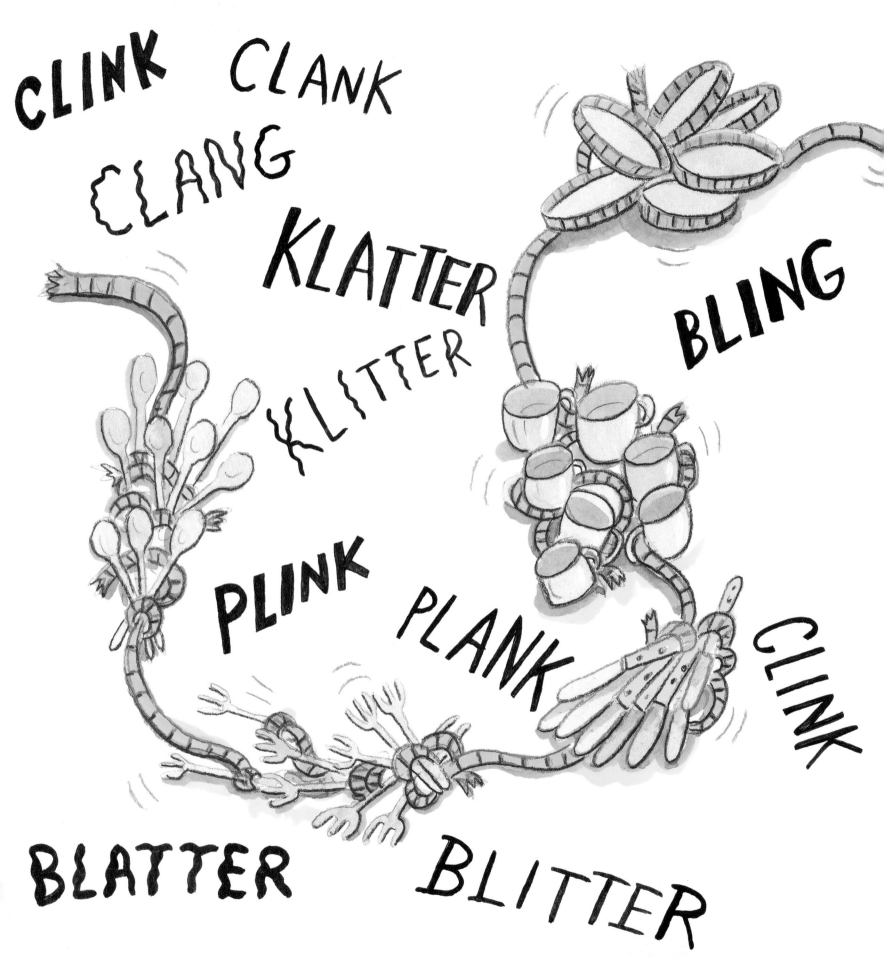

"Look, Iguana!"
cried Tortuga.
"You're not limping
anymore."

Iguana stopped. She looked at her toe and her tail. "I don't believe it," she said. "That noise made me forget my hurt." Iguana grinned. "Untie everything. I'm ready to make *dulces*."

Culebra shook his rattle long and hard. "For a complete cure, Doctor Culebra orders everyone to help."

Iguana measured the cactus butter. Tortuga added sugar and sweet crumbs. Conejo stirred them together.

Then Culebra squiggled and squirmed, shaping the mixture into round *dulces*. Iguana clapped. "We need to thank Doctor Culebra . . ."

". . . who never went to medical school," added Tortuga, "but . . ."

". . . is the best doctor we know," finished Conejo.

Culebra bowed his head. "Enough talk," he said. "Let's eat!"

And they did.

GLOSSARY

Numbers

un, uno*	OON, OON-oh	one
dos	DOSE	two
tres	TRACE	three
cuatro	KWA-troh	four
cinco	SIN-coh	five
seis	SAYSSS	six
siete	see-EHH-tay	seven
ocho	OH-choh	eight
nueve	new-EH-vay	nine
diez	dee-ESS	ten

* When the number one is used as an adjective (such as "one rolling pin"), it is always *un*. When counting, the correct word is *uno*.

Other Words in Spanish

conejo	co-NAY-ho	rabbit
culebra	cu-LAY-brah	snake
dulces	DOOL-says	candies
tortuga	tor-TU-gah	tortoise

RECIPE

Iguana's Cactus Butter *Dulces*

INGREDIENTS
$1/2$ cup cactus butter ($1/2$ stick melted butter and $1/4$ cup peanut butter make a tasty substitute, but ask an adult to help melt the butter)

$2/3$ cup graham cracker crumbs

1 cup plus 2 tablespoons powdered sugar

DIRECTIONS
Using your hands, mix all the ingredients together. Then shape the mixture into one-inch round balls.

Makes one dozen

1 un, uno

rolling pin

2 dos

kettles

3 tres

skillets

4 cuatro

pots

5 cinco

pans